For Avery and Everett
Who love snuggles and cuddles the most.

Love,
Mama

Publisher's Cataloging-in-Publication Data

Names: Ryan, Charlie Eve, author
Title: Blue cat / by Charlie Eve Ryan.
Description: New York, NY: Starberry Books, an imprint of Kane Press, Inc., 2019.
Summary: A young cat goes about its very cat-like day when a sound in the distance
sparks an exploration.
Identifiers: LCCN 2018965800 | ISBN 9781635921342 (Hardcover) | 9781635921359 (ebook)
Subjects: LCSH Cats–Juvenile fiction. | CYAC Cats–Fiction. | BISAC JUVENILE FICTION / Animals / Cats
Classification: LCC PZ7.1 R94 Blu 2019 | DDC [E]–dc23

Library of Congress Control Number: 2018965800

10 9 8 7 6 5 4 3 2 1

First published in the United States of America in 2019
by StarBerry Books, an imprint of Kane Press, Inc.

Printed in China

StarBerry Books is a registered trademark of Kane Press, Inc.

Book Design: Pamela Darcy-Demski

Visit us online at www.kanepress.com

 Like us on Facebook
facebook.com/kanepress

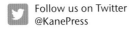 Follow us on Twitter
@KanePress

BLUE CAT

by charlie eve ryan

🍓StarBerry Books
New York

Blue Cat Lounges.

Blue Cat
stretches.

BLUE CAT SWATS.

BLUE CAT JUMPS,

SPLASHES,
ALMOST CRASHES.

BLUE CAT PURRS.

Blue Cat listens.

BLUE CAT PEEKS.

BLUE CAT SNEAKS.

BLUE CAT CREEPS.

Blue Cat POUNCES!

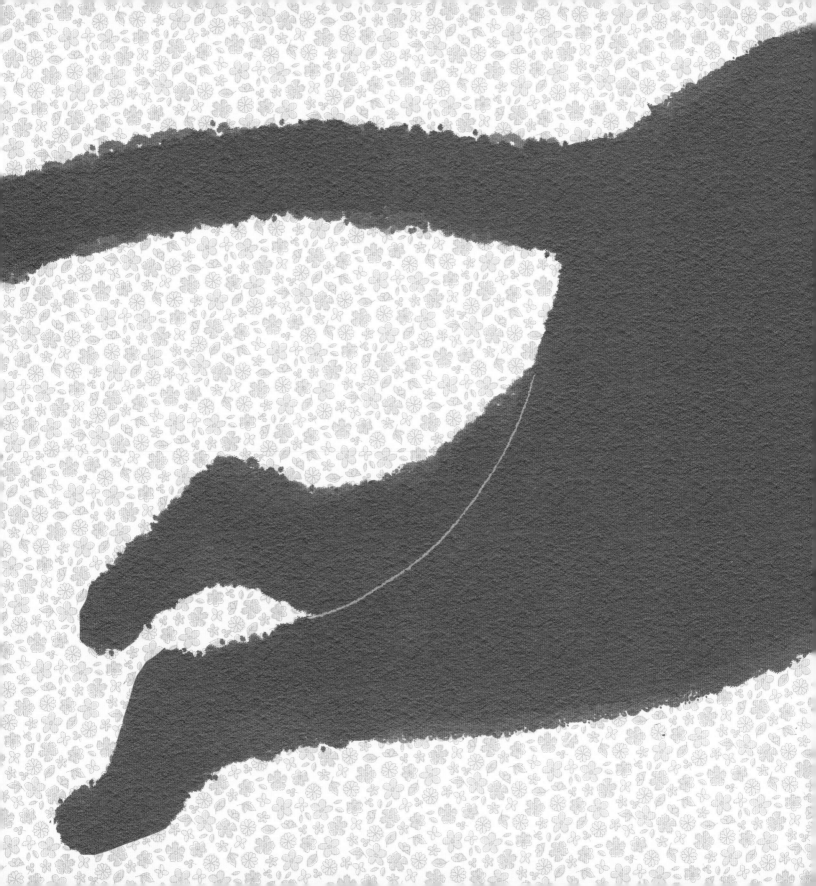

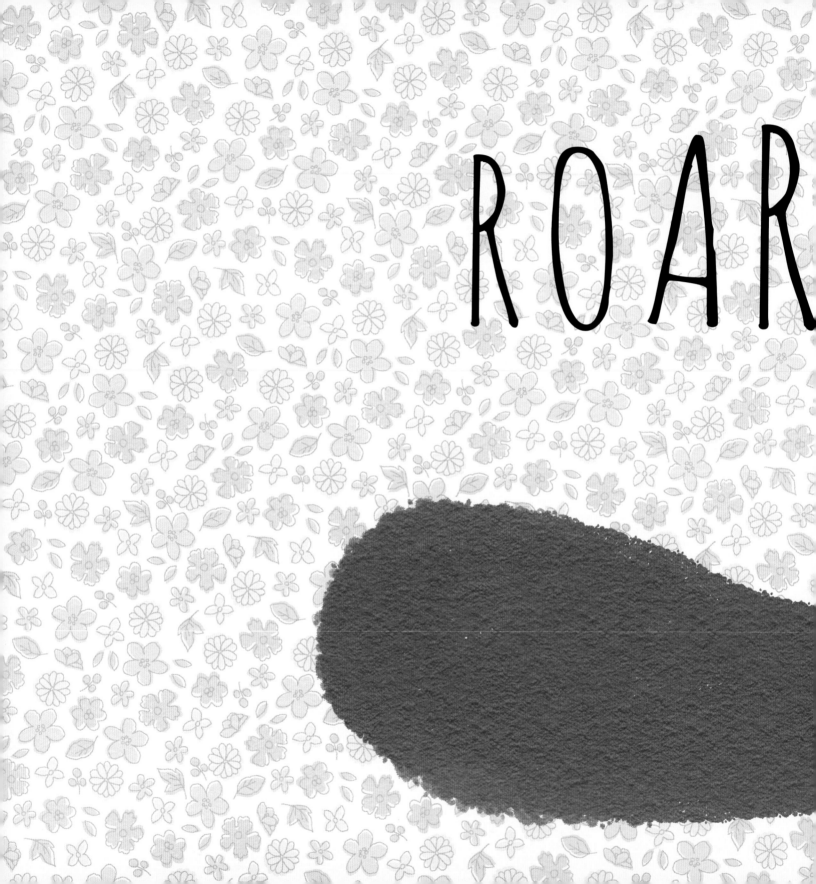

ROAR

Blue Cat snuggles.

MAMA CAT CUDDLES.

31192021810757